Dear Parents:

Congratulations! Your child is taking the first steps on an exciting journey. The destination? Independent reading!

STEP INTO READING® will help your child get there. The program offers five steps to reading success. Each step includes fun stories and colorful art or photographs. In addition to original fiction and books with favorite characters, there are Step into Reading Non-Fiction Readers, Phonics Readers and Boxed Sets, Sticker Readers, and Comic Readers—a complete literacy program with something to interest every child.

Learning to Read, Step by Step!

Ready to Read   Preschool–Kindergarten
• big type and easy words • rhyme and rhythm • picture clues
For children who know the alphabet and are eager to begin reading.

Reading with Help   Preschool–Grade 1
• basic vocabulary • short sentences • simple stories
For children who recognize familiar words and sound out new words with help.

Reading on Your Own   Grades 1–3
• engaging characters • easy-to-follow plots • popular topics
For children who are ready to read on their own.

Reading Paragraphs   Grades 2–3
• challenging vocabulary • short paragraphs • exciting stories
For newly independent readers who read simple sentences with confidence.

Ready for Chapters   Grades 2–4
• chapters • longer paragraphs • full-color art
For children who want to take the plunge into chapter books but still like colorful pictures.

STEP INTO READING® is designed to give every child a successful reading experience. The grade levels are only guides; children will progress through the steps at their own speed, developing confidence in their reading.

Remember, a lifetime love of reading starts with a single step!

Manufactured under license granted to AMEET Sp. z o.o. by the LEGO Group.

AMEET Sp. z o.o.
Nowe Sady 6, 94–102 Łódz—Poland
ameet@ameet.eu
www.ameet.eu

www.LEGO.com

Published in the United States by Random House Children's Books, a division of Penguin Random House LLC, 1745 Broadway, New York, NY 10019, and in Canada by Penguin Random House Canada Limited, Toronto.

Step into Reading, Random House, and the Random House colophon are registered trademarks of Penguin Random House LLC.

Visit us on the Web!
StepIntoReading.com
rhcbooks.com

Educators and librarians, for a variety of teaching tools, visit us at RHTeachersLibrarians.com

ISBN 978-0-593-48378-7 (trade)
ISBN 978-0-593-48379-4 (lib. bdg.)
ISBN 978-0-593-48380-0 (ebook)

Printed in the United States of America
10 9 8 7 6 5 4 3 2 1

Costume Capers

by Steve Foxe

based on the story by Kelly McKain

illustrated by AMEET Studio

Random House 🏠 New York

BEEP!
BEEP!
BEEP!

Mayor Fleck's alarm clock blared.

"Good thing I got

a full night's rest," he said.

"I have so much work to do

before the big Halloween party."

Mayor Fleck jumped out of bed
to start his very busy day.
But something felt . . . wrong.
"My corn outfit!" he cried.
"I never take it off!"
It was gone.

Mayor Fleck put on
the only other suit he owned
and rushed to Town Hall.
Planning the Halloween party
couldn't wait.

But his assistant, Carol,

stopped him at the door.

"Excuse me, sir," she said.

"The mayor isn't in yet."

"I am the mayor!"

he shouted.

"Don't you recognize me?"

Carol squinted at the mayor.
Without his corn suit,
she really didn't recognize him!
Neither did Carol's daughter,
Madison.

"Mommy, who is this
strange man?" she asked.
Carol frowned and looked
closer and closer, until . . .
She gasped. "ARGH! It *is* you!
But, sir, you don't *look* like you!"

Carol wasn't the only one who had trouble recognizing Mayor Fleck.

At the new construction site, no one would work until the "real" mayor showed up to sign off on the permits.

"Nice costume, buddy,"
the foreman joked.
"It'll be a real hit
at the Halloween party."

It only got worse
as the day went on.
At the new shopping center,
they wouldn't let Mayor Fleck
cut the ceremonial ribbon,
so they couldn't start working!

And at the opening

of the hospital's new wing,

the doctors thought

Mayor Fleck was just

a confused patient

who had bonked his head.

Carol was getting worried.
"If no one believes
you're the mayor,
you can't plan the party!"

Then Madison had an idea.
"It's almost Halloween—
you just need a costume!
That way everyone will
recognize you."

Mayor Fleck put on

the airplane outfit

Madison had found for him.

"What does this button do?"

he asked with a smile.

Uh-oh!

The propeller started to spin,

and the mayor flew up in the air!

WHOOSH!

"Heeeeelp!" he cried

as he shot across the room

and right out the window.

Mayor Fleck crash-landed
on Harl the Handyman's bicycle!
"Thanks for breaking my fall,"
the mayor said as he
took off the airplane costume.

"Happy to help, flying stranger,"
Harl replied.

He didn't recognize the mayor!

Mayor Fleck explained the situation,

and Harl had the perfect solution.

"You can borrow my tutu!" he said.

At his office, Mayor Fleck realized
the tutu wasn't right.
And to make matters worse,
his pen suddenly turned
into a banana!

He started to panic.

How could he get his work done

for the Halloween party

if no one believed

he was the mayor?

Just then, Fire Chief Freya McCloud
climbed through his office window.
"Try this on for size,"
  she said, handing Mayor Fleck
  a ninja costume and a set of nunchucks.

But the nunchucks slipped right out
of his hands and flew across the room.
"All this smashing is distracting!" he cried.
"This outfit is not helpful for my work."

"Have no fear—Duke DeTain is here!"

the LEGO® City top cop shouted,

entering through the window

and rolling over the mayor's desk.

"We'll find Mayor Fleck

a more colorful costume

to wear to the party!"

Mayor Fleck felt that something
very strange
was going on.
Where had Duke
come from?
And how had his pen
turned into a banana?

Before Mayor Fleck could
figure out what was happening,
Madison and her friends arrived
with more costumes.

His brain started to boggle.

"Stop this! No more!" he shouted.

No one listened.

There was a whole

avalanche of costumes!

"Help!" wailed the mayor.

"This is scarier than any

Halloween movie marathon!

It's a nightmare!"

BEEP! BEEP! BEEP!

The mayor recognized that sound.

It was his alarm clock!

He gasped.

"It really *had* been a nightmare,"
he said.

"I would never wear

such silly costumes in real life.

And no wonder those weird

things were happening!"

06:00

Best of all, Mayor Fleck's
corn suit was right where
he'd left it: on his body.
"This is the perfect costume
for the Halloween party . . . and
for every other day of the year!"